CHOOSE YOUR OWN ADVENTURE®
NIGHTMARE

EIGHTH GRADE
WITCH

BY C. E. SIMPSON

ILLUSTRATED BY GABHOR UTOMO

CHOOSECO
WAITSFIELD, VERMONT

Eighth Grade Witch artwork, design, and text
©2014 Chooseco LLC, Waitsfield, Vermont.
All Rights Reserved.

Illustrated by: Gabhor Utomo
Book design: Stacey Boyd, Big Eyedea Visual Design

For information regarding permission, write to:

CHOOSECO

P.O. Box 46
Waitsfield, Vermont 05673
www.cyoa.com

ISBN 10 1-937133-45-1
ISBN 13 978-1-937133-45-0

Published simultaneously in the United States and Canada

Printed in Canada

9 8 7 6 5 4 3 2 1

Choose

"These books are like games. Sometimes the choice seems like it will solve everything, but you wonder if it's a trap."

Matt Harmon, age 11

"I think you'd call this a book for active readers, and I am definitely an active reader!"

Ava Kendrick, age 11

"You decide your own fate, but your fate is still a surprise."

Chun Tao Lin, age 10

"Come on in this book if you're crazy enough! One wrong move and you're a goner!"

Ben Curley, age 9

"You can read *Choose Your Own Adventure* books so many wonderful ways. You could go find your dog or follow a unicorn."

Celia Lawton, 11

To my parents.

BEWARE and WARNING!

This book is different from other books.

You and YOU ALONE are in charge of what happens in this story.

There are dangers, choices, adventures, and consequences. YOU must use all of your wits and much of your keen intelligence. The wrong decision could end in disaster—even death. But, don't despair. At any time, YOU can go back and make another choice, alter the path of your story, and change its result.

Your parents are demonologists by profession. And you're happy in your creepy new home—even if it would give most other people nightmares. But when you start your eighth grade year at a new school in Graves End, Brooklyn, chilling visions of the house's haunted past overtake settling in to a new life. What's more, the ghosts are very familiar. Are you the victim of new girl pranks, organized by a local coven obsessed with the mythic history of your house? Or have these witches been dormant for a long time, waiting for you in particular to finally arrive?

You wake with a jolt as your family car comes to a halt. "We're here, Rabbit," your mother says from the front seat. "New home sweet home!"

Where are you again? you wonder sleepily.

Then you remember. You are at your family's new house on Cherry Tree Lane in Graves End, Brooklyn.

You roll your window down and take a look. The house is huge! It looms over you, blocking out the setting sun. You grab your camera and snap a photo of it.

"Look at all these school trees!" your dad says. That's what he calls trees that are changing color. You shiver in the chilly October air. Something about this house doesn't feel quite right to you.

"I can't believe we're moving to a haunted house the day before Halloween," you joke.

You just turned thirteen, and you really did not want to leave all your friends and start a new school in eighth grade, especially because this year you were head of the photo club. You didn't even get to have a party because you were moving.

Turn to the next page.

2

You slump down in your seat and stroke Teacup your white cat, who's sitting at your feet. Your parents want to start fresh after the accident, but Grave's End sounds more like the end of the line.

Then you see your parents smiling at each other in the rear view mirror and you decide to go along with it. You get out of the car and grab the biggest bag you can find and say, "Last one inside is a rotten egg!"

Your mom and dad run up the front steps with you. Your dad unlocks the door and it creaks open. Everyone takes a deep breath.

"It just needs a little love and care," your mom says as the four of you peer in. White sheets cover antique furniture and a dusty, dank smell hangs in the air.

"Teacup!" you yell as she bounds into the house and up the stairs. You drop your bags and run after her. She disappears down a long shadowy hallway and through an open door. "Teacup?" you whisper. You push the door open and spy two little white paws under the bed. You snap a photo of her and look around the room.

Turn to page 4.

4

The room is gigantic. It has a canopy bed, a fire-place, and a chandelier. The house came furnished, and you can see why your mom thought this was a selling point. *I could get used to this*, you think and flop on the bed. Teacup has found the best room in the house. Smart cat.

You open the curtains and a huge cloud of dust hits you in the face. You throw open the window and take a deep breath.

"Achoo!" you sneeze so loudly that your dad hears you.

"Dusty up there?" he shouts from behind the trunk of the car.

"You said it!" you reply mid-sneeze. Your eyes start to water and everything goes blurry for a second. You are about to ask your dad to bring up your red backpack when you look out the window. Instead of your dad you see a man with a scar rummaging through your car.

"Hey!" you yell. "What are you doing?" You run downstairs and out to the car but the intruder has disappeared. Nothing seems to be taken but there is a dirty hand print on your backpack.

Go on to the next page.

You look through your bag to check that your other film and lenses are still safe. At that moment, a girl and a boy about your age ride up on their bikes and stop at the end of your short driveway.

"Hey, we're your neighbors," says the girl who has the same red backpack as you. She drops her bag next to yours and extends her hand. "I'm Astrid and this is my younger brother Felix."

Felix murmurs "hello," but looks past you at the house.

"Hi," you say. You look past Astrid and up and down the street.

"Are you looking for something?" asks Astrid.

"I just thought I saw someone," you say. You are surprised to see Astrid smiling mysteriously.

"Lots of weirdos in this neighborhood," Astrid says, and her green eyes glint. Before you can ask her anything else your mom sticks her head out of the kitchen window.

"Do you kids want some lemonade?" she asks warmly.

"Oh, no we can't right now. But thanks," Astrid says, giving a friendly wave.

Turn to the next page.

6

The whole time Felix's green eyes have been fixed intently on your house, as if he's trying to memorize each ivy-covered inch.

"Haunted!" he suddenly sputters. "Your house is haunted."

"What?" you say. You feel a chill creep up your back.

"This house is cursed!" he screams and shoves you hard in the stomach.

"Felix!" Astrid exclaims. "Are you crazy?"

She grabs her red bag and looks at you apologetically. "I'm sorry, he doesn't take well to strangers," she says as she pulls her brother away. They push off on their bikes. You grab your red bag and follow your mom into the house.

After a late dinner you decide to take some photos of the new house. You go to grab your bag from the kitchen but it looks a little different. For one, it's lighter and the hand print is gone. You feel around for your camera, but it's not there.

"Uh-oh. This is Astrid's bag," you say. Suddenly you hear a crackling noise coming from the backpack.

Go on to the next page.

You open the bag and pull out a walkie-talkie.

"Alley Cat to Nightshade and Fang. Do you read me?" the walkie-talkie crackles. "Nightshade...do you read me? Astrid, are you there? Are we a go on mission TP Cherry Tree?"

"Fang to all! I think we should table TP-ing the house on Cherry Tree Lane," the walkie-talkie warbles. "Fang to Alley Cat, Astrid is the only way we know how to get into that stupid house anyway."

"Alley Cat to Fang, it's Trick Night and you know what that means. If we don't TP the house on Cherry Tree Lane, the seniors are gonna egg us. We need to act soon."

The walkie-talkie goes dead and you look out your window. The street is dark except for the lights in two different houses signaling each other.

You look at the walkie-talkie unsure of what to do next. Your finger hovers over the red "talk" button. Should you say something, or continue to listen?

If you decide to keep listening, turn to page 8.

If you decide to press "talk," turn to page 11.

8

You decide to keep listening to the walkie-talkie. It sparks to life.

"Alley Cat to Fang, I am calling an emergency meeting of the Deadly Nightshades! Midnight at the foot of the black tree in Lockworm Cemetery. Bring your Ouija board! Over!"

The walkie-talkie goes dead. You look up "black tree" and "Lockworm Cemetery" on your computer. It is very close to your house. You make yourself a map. Then you open Astrid's bag to look for more clues.

You pour the backpack out and sift through its contents. She has an old leather notebook with a lock on it. Hmmm. As you're trying to open it, a Polaroid slips out. You freeze. It's a photo of you leaning out of your car window. On the back of the Polaroid, it says, "time of arrival: 6:13 PM." Now you're starting to get nervous.

Astrid has been watching you, but why?

If you decide that you need some help to figure out what Astrid is up to, turn to page 20.

If you decide to investigate Astrid first, turn to page 33.

If you decide to go to the cemetery, turn to page 38.

You jump out of your seat and print the photos of the Emerald Coven. You snatch them from the printer and stuff them into your backpack.

On your way out the librarian gives you a grin and taps her green finger nails on her desk.

The hallway is loud and chaotic. For a moment you are lost in the crowd. You catch a glimpse of the janitor out of the corner of your eye. You recognize the white crown-like scar from the bushes.

"Hey!" you shout. "Do I know you?" He turns and smiles at you. You walk up to him slowly. Only when you are standing close to him do you realize that it is Peter! He smiles and gestures to his nametag that reads: "Peter."

"I researched your note," you whisper and take out the photos. Peter shakes his head and cautiously glances to his left and right. He motions for you to follow him and opens the door to the room where he keeps cleaning supplies. It is very dark inside.

If you decide to go with Peter, turn to page 34.

If you decide to bolt, go to page 71.

10

Your parents follow you back to your house. Before they can ask you any questions, you announce that you are going to bed.

The next day you wake up early for school. You wouldn't normally be nervous--you're a first day veteran--but Astrid's threats are making you anxious. The school is typical looking, except for the Halloween decorations. Your first class is history with Mrs. Nussbaum. Mrs. Nussbaum is a large woman. She wears a dress with a high collar.

"In honor of Halloween we will be studying local legends, most notably that of the famous Graves End witch Prudence Deadly. She was an expert herbologist and potions master, and legend tells of a witch coven in this very area lead by Prudence Deadly herself! Contrary to the Salem witches, the New York witches were not part of human society and often communicated in coded language."

It reminds you of the gibberish on Peter's note last night. After Mrs. Nussbaum's class you head to the library to look up the code. Could it have something to do with Prudence Deadly?

*If you decide to ask the librarian,
turn to page 14.*

*If you decide to use the internet,
turn to page 26.*

You press the red talk button and say: "Nightshade to all! Mayday! Mayday! We have been breached." There is a long pause and then you feel that chill on your neck.

"Who knows about us, Nightshade?"

"The neighbors found my walkie."

"Neighbors?!" Fang shrieks. "We should meet at the black tree in Lockworm Cemetery to plan!"

"Alley Cat to all, see you at midnight, okay Nightshade?" You wait for a moment and then respond. There is a long pause. Your hands are shaking a little.

"Alley Cat to Nightshade, you sound different. Who is this?" Alley Cat asks.

"If you come anywhere near this house tonight you'll regret it," you say.

"Who are you?" Fang whimpers.

"I am the Black Cat. Stay away from the house on Cherry Tree Lane."

There is no response from Fang or Alley Cat. You scared them off, for now. But what should you do next?

If you decide to go to the cemetery, turn to page 12.

If you decide you have scared them away and go to sleep, turn to page 75.

12

You decide to go to Lockworm Cemetery and scare them for good. You look it up on your computer. It's very close to your house. You draw yourself a map. Unfortunately there is no way for you to find the black tree. Maybe Astrid and the Deadly Nightshades can show you the way?

You check the time. It is half past eleven. Without waking your parents, you sneak downstairs and out the back door. It is a chilly night. As you cross the back yard the cracked faces of broken statues watch you. You step carefully to avoid disturbing them.

You make a right down your neighbor's alley and turn down the next dark street. Eventually you reach a crooked sign that says "Lockworm" in black lettering. You walk along the iron fence until you see a gate. It's locked but you find a small hole in the fence. You crawl through and look around. Lockworm is very old, and most of the mausoleums are covered in thick moss. It is almost midnight. You decide to hide and wait for the Deadly Nightshades.

Turn to page 55.

Just as you are about to turn to run home, you hear Edith's voice.

"Felix! Felix! Where are you?" There is a worried tone in her voice. Suddenly Felix rushes out of the bushes and tackles you. He's wearing a cape made of dead rabbits and kittens, with an animal skull on his head.

"I'm a monster!" he screams and tears at your sweater. Felix howls at you and tries to scratch your face as Edith pulls him off of you.

"I said monster time was over for today!" she states firmly. Edith drags Felix back into the house, apologizing profusely to you over her shoulder.

Your mom and dad emerge from the house looking concerned. "And we were worried they would think *we* were strange," your mom says under her breath as you return home.

You settle in to Cherry Tree Lane and never see Felix again. Later, you hear from your parents that Edith had to commit Felix to an institution for violently disturbed children.

The End

14

You see the librarian and decide to ask her for help. She is sitting at her desk, snapping her gum and reading *The Crucible*.

"Can I access your card catalog?" you ask, eyeing her emerald lizard brooch. She sighs and looks up.

"What are you looking for?" She snatches Peter's code out of your hand without asking. She snaps her fingers and looks at you. "This is a very special book," she says. "You can locate it using the card catalog in the basement." She motions to the old metal door behind her desk.

You walk down three flights of stairs. The basement looks as if it has been left untouched for many years. The card catalog sits in gray wooden drawers.

You take out Peter's code and open a drawer marked "2W," and finally locate 2WRBT1. The card's edges are burned. It directs you to the back of the stacks. You come across *Possession for Beginners* and *Creatures of the East River*.

Then "2WRBT1" is under your fingers. You grasp and pull at the book, and a shiver runs up your spine.

Turn to page 30.

Your dad takes Officer Treacle on a tour of the house to secure it. At the basement door Officer Treacle clicks his flashlight on and hops down the stairs. You and your parents return to the kitchen and continue unpacking. Suddenly, you hear a commotion coming from the basement.

"Help! Help! Get me out!" Officer Treacle yells. You and your parents run to the basement door and open it. Officer Treacle leaps out of the basement. He is covered in green slime and red intestines!

"I'm free! I'm free!" he yells, and runs into the wall by the top of the stairs, knocking himself out. You and your parents are shocked. You stand over him as your mom calls 9-1-1. Suddenly, Officer Treacle grabs your ankle. You scream!

"I ate my way out," he whispers. "I can still feel the web tightening around me." He takes a deep breath and drifts off. Then he starts to shake, still holding onto your ankle.

"Mom!" you scream. Officer Treacle trembles and his mouth opens. "Mom!" you yell even louder. Hundreds of tiny, black, screaming spiders pour out of his mouth.

The End

18

You hand over the backpack and Officer Treacle sits down at the table. You show him the Polaroid and tell him about the walkie-talkie conversation in more detail. He begins to look through the evidence carefully. He breaks open Astrid's diary and smiles. You notice a strange green flash in his eyes. Officer Treacle looks at you curiously.

"I wonder if you're the one I should interrogate," he says and smiles. You look at him quizzically and then the phone rings. You get up to answer it.

"Hello?" you ask.

"Hello, this is the NYPD. We just wanted to let you know we have dispatched a car and it will be there any minute." You freeze.

"But someone is already here...." you say. You look back but Officer Treacle is gone, and so is Astrid's bag!

The End

One advantage to having parents who are professional ghost hunters is that no question seems too weird. The only problem is that this neighbor situation feels scarily similar to the one you just left.

You don't remember much from that night. Your parents had been leading an exorcism and something went very wrong. Most neighborhoods don't take kindly to ghost hunters to begin with. Trouble with your new neighbors on Cherry Tree Lane could bring the whole ugly story to the surface.

Maybe it's better to get the police involved immediately instead?

If you decide to go to your parents first and show them Astrid's Polaroid, go on to the next page.

If you decide to just call the police instead, turn to page 77.

You find your parents downstairs unpacking their ghost-hunting equipment. You hand them Astrid's polaroid.

"I accidentally switched backpacks with that girl Astrid from across the street," you begin. "They are identical. The only reason I noticed was because her walkie-talkie went off. She is planning to break into our house tonight with her friends and TP everything!"

Your parents exchange a quick glance.

"You mean cover everything with toilet paper?" your mom asks.

You nod.

"It's Trick Night tonight," you remind her.

Your parents listen with grave faces. Your mom puts down her Geiger counter.

"Well, we're going to have a talk with Astrid's parents," your dad says.

You were afraid of this but he's right. The three of you cross your new street, Astrid's backpack in hand, and climb the steps to her front door.

"They have a Christmas wreath on their door on Halloween?" you ask quietly as your dad raps on the door.

Turn to page 23.

Astrid's mother answers after a few knocks, looking harried. She is a very tall, pale woman in her fifties with long gray hair and long green nails. She looks like one of the skinny crooked trees in your yard.

"Hello, how can I help you?" she asks. Then she sees Astrid's bag. "Oh, I recognize that! You must be the new neighbors! I am Astrid's mother, Edith."

"We are the Hawthorns," your mom says. "Can we come in for a moment?"

"Well, now isn't a great time, actually. Maybe we can do something this week?" Edith says as she grabs the bag, shutting the door slightly.

Your dad puts his foot in the door and says, "I am afraid this can't wait."

He quickly recounts your story. Edith smiles.

"You must have heard about your place?" she asks. Your parents look at each other. Edith explains that your house is home to many ghost sightings, dating as far back as the late 18th century when it was built. "A notorious witch named Prudence Deadly used a secret room in your basement to perform her evil rituals. Legend says that the spirits of her victims still haunt your house."

Turn to the next page.

Edith tickles your parents' demonologist funny bones. Soon they are sitting down to tea and chatting like old friends. As you listen, Astrid comes up behind you and whispers, "Those ghosts won't be able to get you because by the end of school tomorrow you'll be finished."

Then Felix tugs your sleeve, and adds, "Everyone who moves into that house disappears because of Prudence Deadly."

"Felix, get out of here, you freak," Astrid hisses.

"You'll see…." Felix whispers.

"You better watch it," Astrid says mockingly. "You won't see us coming and in that freaky house you won't know if it's us or the ghosts." She laughs maniacally.

"I'm not afraid of ghosts!" you say and walk out the front door.

You start out the front gate when you hear a rustling in the bushes. Then the tall bush next to you moves. Both bushes move again. A hand emerges from the bush and beckons you nearer.

You step back and look around. Your parents are still inside. Is this Astrid or Felix playing a trick on you?

If you decide to go home, turn to page 13.

If you decide to answer the hand and explore the bushes, turn to page 29.

You decide to keep researching and come across a website that says the "Deadly Nightshades" are a cult that worships Prudence Deadly. The blog is mostly about different potions that Prudence Deadly used on her victims. Some of them are pranks, like the "Sunflower Scale Serum," which gives its victim lizard scales for one day. Then there are stronger spells like "Cherry Lane Pie" that sucks the powers out of the victim.

Farther down the page, you find an article listing every witch in the Emerald coven. You scroll some more and your heart starts to race as you recognize some of the younger faces: Edith, Mrs. Nussbaum, and the librarian.

That's when you hear a creak behind you. Before you can turn around you feel two thin hands closing around your nose and mouth. The last sound you hear is the librarian smacking her gum in your ear.

"Shhhhh, my pretty…" she whispers and everything goes black.

The End

26

You decide to use a computer for research and find a free monitor in the computer lab. You type out "2WRBT1," press return, and wait. Nothing comes up after a few seconds. On a whim, you search your street name, "Cherry Tree Lane." Jackpot!

You scroll down a webpage with hundreds of links to hauntings in Brooklyn. You randomly click on a link. It takes you to www.hiddenhaunts.org. Your house is not exactly a "hidden haunt." It's more like a notoriously-haunted mansion. So that's why your parents were so eager to move.

You read one very chilling legend about your house. Every family that has lived in the house on Cherry Tree Lane has gone missing, always under mysterious circumstances.

You look up Prudence Deadly and find photos of the "Deadly Nightshades," one modern group's take on Prudence Deadly's original "Emerald Coven." There are photos of girls wearing cloaks and smiling while holding lizards. The lunch bell rings. You jump as if someone snuck up behind you.

If you decide to leave the library and go to the cafeteria, turn to page 9.

If you decide to keep researching, turn to page 25.

You leap into the bushes yelling, "Gotcha!" Suddenly, you are knocked to the ground, face to face with a big slobbering dog! The dog growls menacingly and presses his bear-like paws into your chest.

Then you hear a quick clap. The dog lets up and steps off of you. The guy who was rummaging through your car looms over you. You try to move but the dog growls. The guy is not that much older than you, you guess about eighteen years old. The scar on his face is white and curls around his head.

"Help!" you yell but your parents are still inside. He gets closer to you until you are face to face. He smiles with his crooked, yellow teeth. You look away and feel the dog's tongue lapping at your leg. He puts a note in your hand and runs off. His dog follows.

The note reads: "My name is Peter. I'm sorry if I scared you, but I'm mute and needed to get your attention. I can help you find answers." The last line of the note is just gibberish: "2WRBT1."

"Hey! Rabbit! Where are you?" your dad calls. You bolt out of the bushes and past your parents.

Turn to page 10.

30

You read the title out loud: "Murdoch's Myths and Local Legends: Tenth Edition." You open to the table of contents and your eye lands on a chapter entitled *Graves End Greats: Prudence Deadly, Zora Belladonna, and the Legend of the Emerald Coven.*

You continue reading out loud, "At the height of the Industrial Revolution, the Emerald Coven was most active. To curb New York City's progression and further deterioration of outlying woodlands and habitats, Prudence Deadly tried to wage war on humans with an ancient relic called 'Gaia's Claw.' This relic gave its owner power over all the flora and fauna of Earth. This caused a rift between Zora and Prudence because Prudence had to imprison her parents to gain the relic."

You see a drawing of a gnarled claw with the caption "Gaia's Claw" and a portrait of Prudence Deadly.

"She looks just like Astrid!" you gasp and shut the book. The bell is ringing for lunch.

*If you decide to keep reading,
go on to page 31.*

*If you decide to head to the cafeteria,
turn to page 105.*

You can't stop reading now! You turn to the next page and see the words "Cherry Tree Lane House condemned" beside an image of your house during the early 19th century. Prudence Deadly stands in front with her coven. They all wear dark capes.

Next is an image of a newspaper article that reads:

Prudence Deadly, leader of the Emerald Coven, was arrested on charges of Arson and Kidnapping yesterday. The notorious witch used ritualistic possession to gain power and gather followers that she brainwashed and kept in hiding in the mansion on Cherry Tree Lane in Graves End, Brooklyn. Authorities are considering condemning the building because of the atrocities that occurred on the premises.

Suddenly, you hear another ringing, but much louder this time. The sprinklers go on and start to soak everything around you. The fire alarm blares in your ears. You begin to feel hot, and you notice flames licking at the base of the stacks where you found your book. You grab the book and dash toward the emergency exit at the end of the stacks. Three flights up, the door in front of you says MAIN LIBRARY. Should you go in? Or continue upward?

If you decide to continue up the stairs, turn to page 32.

If you decide go into the library, turn to page 106.

You continue up another flight. There is an unmarked door, and you burst through. You've stumbled into the main hallway. The central stairwell is flooding because of the sprinklers and you almost slip a few times. All the students have been ushered out of the building, except for the janitor who stands in the middle of the soaking hallway mopping fruitlessly. He turns to you and your stomach drops.

Your school janitor is young and has a big scar across his head. It's Peter!

"Hello," you say but he just nods. You remember that he cannot speak.

You take out *Murdoch's Myths: Tenth Edition* and hold it up. He smiles and gives you a thumbs up. Then, with water sprinkling all around you, Peter motions you to follow him. He leads you to the room where he keeps cleaning supplies. Inside he pulls a sheet off the wall. It is covered with photos, articles and notes about the Emerald Coven, the Deadly Nightshades, and your house, in the center of it all.

If you decide to trust Peter and stay, turn to page 34.

If you decide to bolt, turn to page 71.

Why is Astrid watching me? you wonder. This house is already weird without having creepy neighbors. *If they break into my house, I'll be ready for them*, you think.

You didn't grow up with ghost-hunter parents for nothing! In your old house, your parents had an elaborate network of motion-sensor and infrared cameras that detected changes in temperature and light. Needless to say, it was not easy getting a midnight snack!

You can use some of their ghost hunting methods to catch the Deadly Nightshades. You scan Astrid's Polaroid. Everything looks fine—the yard, the front door, the window. Wait! You spot a figure with fiery red hair standing at the window of the room you are sitting in right now!

A ghost?!

If you decide to show your parents the ghost in the photo first, turn to page 48.

If you decide to set up some ghost detectors, turn to page 74.

34

Peter turns on a light in the supply closet and pours cleaning supplies into a mop bucket full of dirty water. He takes a false bottom off of a tissue box and takes out a vial of black powder. It dissolves in the bucket with a hiss. The mop bucket begins to glow with a bright blue fizzing light.

Peter opens *Murdoch's Myths* to a page that describes Prudence Deadly's final resting place in a network of catacombs under the Metropolitan Museum of Art. He gestures to the book and then to the bucket. He steps gingerly into the mop bucket and in a flash of blue he disappears.

"Hey!" you cry. "Where did you go?!" At that moment one of Peter's notes floats to the top of the bucket. It reads "Jump in." You take a deep breath and dip your fingers into the bucket and then your arms. The water is warm but you can't feel the bottom. Then you feel something pulling you. You hold your breath and dive in with a splash.

Turn to page 78.

You decide giving your fellow lizard a chance is your only hope.

"Let's wrap our tails, and then you start to dig," he commands. You do as he says. He begins to glow just like the headstone. You see the familiar flash of blue. You feel your arms and legs growing back and your skin returning to normal.

The blue tunnel gets darker and darker until you are tossed onto the floor of the supply closet back at school. You look around. You can still hear students in the hallway. Peter helps you up and the lizard minister leaps onto his shoulder.

"Thank you for reuniting us!" the lizard minister says. Peter smiles. Then he tosses the glowing mop water on you! The blue light flashes again and in an instant you are at home on your bed.

Astrid's bag sits on the floor and the walkie-talkie crackles on your windowsill. You have gone back in time to the night before your first day of school. You are holding the map you made of your neighborhood with Lockworm Cemetery circled in red. This is where Alley Cat and Fang said the Deadly Nightshades would be meeting, and Peter must think you should go if he left you back with your map.

Turn to page 38.

You and Astrid duck into Peter's supply closet. It's pitch black inside. Suddenly someone gives you a shove that knocks you to the ground. The door quickly opens and shuts. The next thing you know you hear Astrid giggling on the other side of the door as she locks it from the outside! You stand and feel around for a light switch and flick it.

The closet is filled from floor to ceiling with crucifixes! "Help! Help!" you scream. The bell rings. You hear footsteps all around you, but no matter how loud you scream, no one can hear you.

You scream until you have no voice left. You bang on the walls, harder and harder until the crucifixes start falling. They cut through the air. "Ouch!" you scream as a sharp silver cross cuts your cheek and draws blood. You stop banging but crucifixes keep falling. The principal finds you the next day, barely alive and clinging to a mop.

Astrid denies everything. But two weeks later, you get revenge. You lure her into your basement with stories of an ancient diary and lock her in. You mean it as a joke, but when you open the door three hours later, she is no longer there. You turn the basement upside down but Astrid is never found.

The End

38

The full moon is so high in the sky that it almost looks light outside. You walk over to your desk and look at the map to the cemetery. The grandfather clock in the hall chimes eleven times.

You listen for the sounds of your parents going to bed. As soon as their door is shut and lights turned out, you grab the map and sneak down the back stairs and out the back door.

It is almost midnight when you reach Lockworm Cemetery. The gate is locked. You walk around the old iron fence until you see an opening you can squeeze through. The white graves seem to go on forever and stand in sharp contrast to the black ground. On your map, the cemetery is shaped like an upside down triangle. You study it and locate the "black tree" in the northeast corner. It should be fairly close. Suddenly you hear footsteps approaching and you duck behind a tombstone.

Two people climb through the fence: a tall woman and a very short man. They walk quickly, heading in your direction. They stop short in front of your hiding place, and the small man throws a duffel bag on the ground with a loud thud. You hold your breath.

Turn to page 40.

"Marty! Are you trying to wake the dead?" the tall woman snaps.

"Sorry, Trix," Marty mumbles. He opens the duffel bag and starts unloading shovels, a crowbar, and plastic bags onto the grass.

"Marty, what are you doing? We're not at the site yet," Trix says, shaking her head.

"Oh, right," Marty says, scratching his head. "Where's the site this time?"

"North side of the cemetery near the black tree. The grave is in the northeast corner," Trix says.

"Then what?" Marty asks sheepishly.

"Then...PAYDAY!" she says and squeezes him. They both grin. "This is going to be a big one Marty. The Boss will be pleased. Remember what happened when he wasn't pleased?" Marty looks at his hand. Two of his fingers are missing.

"Yeah, I remember," Marty mumbles.

Trix grabs a shovel and starts walking. Marty lugs the huge duffel bag behind him.

Who are these people? And what are they doing?

*If you decide to follow Marty and Trix,
go on to the next page.*

If you decide to keep waiting, turn to page 55.

They'll lead me to the black tree, if nothing else, you think as you decide to follow along. Trix and Marty walk in silence. You move from headstone to headstone. After walking awhile, a row of saplings appears against the dark blue sky. There is a fresh grave in the middle of the trees.

"Thank you Ida Turner, loving Wife and Mother," Trix says and sticks her shovel into the mound of fresh dirt.

"Dig this," she orders, and sits on the grave. Marty picks up the shovel. Trix looks up at the stars and murmurs something into the night. After a while, Marty finishes and throws the shovel out of the hole. He grabs the crowbar and you hear the screech of the coffin lid getting pried open.

"Hey! Jackpot!" Marty says. "Bring the flashlight!"

Trix shines the flashlight in and whistles under her breath.

"Newspaper said she died yesterday so we have to work quickly," she says. "Let's pull her out." You freeze. You don't know if you want to see a dead body.

If you decide to run, turn to page 43.

If you decide to stay where you are, turn to page 46.

You do NOT want to see a dead body. You begin to sneak away but you step on a votive candle and it crunches under your sneaker. The glass goes through the bottom of your shoe and you whimper.

"Who's there?" Trix barks. You press yourself against the tombstone and hold your breath. She starts looking behind headstones, one by one.

"What if it's the police?" Marty asks. But Trix ignores him.

"Come out, come out, wherever you are," Trix whispers. You try to run but you can't even walk. She gets closer and closer until she's three tombstones away, then two, then right next to you.

"Ah-ha!" Trix says and pulls you up by the ear.

"Ouch!" you howl as you step on your bad foot.

"What are you doing here you little witch?" Trix demands.

"Yeah! What are you doing here?" Marty asks, climbing out of the grave.

"Please! Let me go! I won't tell anyone," you say pleadingly.

Turn to the next page.

44

"No, you won't tell anyone," she says. "Marty! Pull Ida Turner out of her box. We're taking her with us." Marty does not respond. "Hey, Tiny. Listen up!"

"What did you call me?" Marty asks.

"I called you 'Tiny,' because you have a brain the size of a pea," Trix hisses.

"Don't call me Tiny. That's mean," Marty says.

"Oh, Marty we have more to worry about right now besides your feelings. We have a donor right here. Forget Ida!"

"I thought you said no one would get hurt. Look at her, she's bleeding," he says, eying your foot.

"Tiny, get the shovel!" Trix retorts. She turns and looks into your eyes. Behind her, you see Marty approaching with the shovel. He gets close and then his eyes flash. He brings the shovel back, and you wince. He knocks Trix hard on her back.

"Run!" he says to you.

"Thank you," you say, still in shock. You limp away from the grave and as fast as you can out of the cemetery.

Go on to the next page.

As soon as you get home you call the police and tell them that there was an incident in the northeast corner of Lockworm Cemetery.

The story breaks the next day: "Famous Grave Robbers Caught!" The headline spreads across the front page of the *New York Times*. Trix and Marty were part of an infamous grave-robbing ring that had been eluding the police for years. Your anonymous tip took down the whole gang.

You are a hero! Even if no one knows it except your parents, who ground you for leaving the house after your curfew, without permission, on a school night.

The End

46

What's the harm? They can't see me, you think to yourself. Then, oddly, Trix jumps into the grave with rubber gloves and a saw. You wince as a sound like splitting wood slices through the night air. You realize then that these are not typical grave robbers.

Trix throws the saw out of the grave. It is covered in blood. Then she climbs out, pulling Ida Turner's chest cavity with her.

They're organ thieves!

"Get the blade, Marty," Trix hisses, and he hands her a small knife. She unsheathes the knife and holds it up. Its point flashes in the moonlight. Trix grasps the chest cavity and cuts around each of the body's organs.

"Marty, bring the cooler now."

This is getting worse by the second. You are so terrified you can hardly breathe.

Marty tosses her the cooler from the bag without looking at the body. You gasp as Trix gingerly places each organ into the icy box. After she's finished with the chest cavity, Trix signals Marty to rebury the corpse.

You can't believe what you've just seen. It's so awful that you start to cry softly against the headstone.

Go on to the next page.

You wish you could forget what you just saw. Suddenly the headstone you are leaning against falls over with a clunk! Trix and Marty whip their heads in your direction. Trix grabs the crowbar and walks briskly over to you.

"Hey! Who are you?" she asks. "Actually, it doesn't matter. You won't even remember in a minute." Marty comes up behind you and keeps you from moving. Trix winds up to hit you.

"Help!" you scream. "Help me, Deadly Nightshades!" You see the crowbar zooming toward your face. You wince but there is no impact! You open your eyes and see a huge decaying arm holding the crowbar a few inches from your face.

The arm rips the crowbar out of Trix's hands and grabs her ankles and pulls itself out of the grave. You hear the moans of corpses gathering behind you. Marty lets go and you run but slip into Ida's grave. As soon as you touch her, all of her limbs start to wiggle. You scream. The ribs close over your ankle. You drag the limbs and chest with you and leap out of the grave.

Turn to page 52.

48

"Mom! Dad!" you yell. "Look at this!" You rush down the stairs and bump into your dad, carrying a big box.

"Whoa, there," he says, teetering on the landing.

"Dad! The house is haunted. Look!" You show him the photo. "See, there's someone in my room."

"Honey, we got one!" your dad hollers to your mom. He drops the box. "Unpack the gear—we have to set up the house now."

You go into your parents' office which is half-unpacked. The office floor is crowded with boxes of ghost-hunting equipment.

Go on to the next page.

"First things first: let's get the Geiger counter out and see if we can get any EMF readings," your dad says and picks up two blown up photographs. He pins them to the wall to get them out of the way.

One is a poster of an orb glowing above a dirty mattress. Then there is one that you recognize: the photo of a young boy sitting on a couch. A ghostly hand reaching for him. The hand has green shiny finger nails. You know this photo because it is the reason you had to leave your old house.

Turn to the next page.

The last job your parents had was in your old town. A little boy named John was very sick and his parents didn't know why. He had bruises all over. He was sleepwalking and having terrible nightmares. By the time your parents were hired, it was a serious possession.

They did everything they could, but during the exorcism, when your parents and the family had joined hands and were praying, something terrible happened. John had been levitating over the bed and as the family prayed he slowly drifted down. Then with a deafening crack, the boy's spine snapped in two and he let out a deep wail. Without thinking, the mother broke the circle and in that instant the creature took her son.

Of course, his parents blamed your parents. The next night, your neighbors assembled in front of your house with torches. The flames caught on the oak tree in your yard and spread. You and your parents grabbed what you could and sped off. You've been living in a motel for weeks trying to find a new home.

"Why do you have that picture on the wall?" you ask.

Go on to the next page.

"We don't want to forget what happened that tragic day," your mom replies, coming in. "There are a few things we didn't tell you about this house," she says and takes a deep breath. "This house has been haunted for centuries. We are here to figure out by whom."

"We were lucky to find this place for the price we did," your dad says. "We're doing the community a service. It's something your mom and I need to do after what happened."

Before you can say anything there's a crash from downstairs. You and your parents rush into the living room and gasp when you see that the the white sheets that covered the furniture have all been ripped to shreds. Suddenly all the windows shatter simultaneously.

"Something wants us to leave," your dad says.

You and your parents stand frozen. Little do you know that no resident has ever escaped Cherry Tree Lane. But you'll find out soon!

The End

52

Back above Ida's grave, the scene is terrifying. Marty is being pulled apart by an old woman in a nighty and Trix is trying to fight off two other corpses. Then Ida gets her revenge. Her arms close around what is left of Marty and she drags him into her grave.

You swing your leg out from under you and Ida Turner's chest cavity flies into the air. Smack! It lands onto Trix's head and eats her alive like a Venus Fly Trap. Blood splatters everywhere as you cover your face.

When you uncover your eyes the night is silent and tranquil. You walk away slowly toward the entrance of the cemetery.

"Was that real?" you wonder aloud. Then you hear something behind you. It is Ida's head.

"Thank you, young witch," the red lips say and heavily made-up eyes wink.

It was real.

You shriek and run home the rest of the way.

The End

You are so curious about what's going to happen next you can't stop watching now. Astrid lights a black candle and pours the hot wax around the frog and the objects. She picks up the frog and holds it above her head. Fang and Alley Cat watch transfixed. Astrid opens her mouth and the frog begins to struggle. You watch in horror.

The frog wiggles his legs as Astrid opens her mouth and brings him down slowly.

"With this offering I do possess thee…" In a flash, she bites down on the frog. She coughs and sputters, spraying frog blood everywhere. You duck as it sprays against the glass on the window. The blood pours out of the frog and extinguishes the candle. Fang screams and turns on her flashlight.

"No lights!" screams Astrid and in the moonlight she paints the objects and her face with the frog blood. Astrid exhales into the red light and a cloud of ectoplasm in the shape of three lizards escapes her lips. The lizards rise like smoke out of the cabin. Two of the lizards veer off in the direction of your house and the third spins around and flies directly into your mouth. Everything goes black. You are powerless against Prudence Deadly.

The End

You duck behind a mausoleum to stay out of view. After a few minutes you see Astrid climb through the hole in the fence followed by two hooded figures who must be Fang and Alley Cat. You follow them.

"Fang, pick up the pace. We have a long walk," Astrid says as Fang lags behind looking at a headstone.

"Okay," she sighs and gallops to catch up.

They walk in single file for a while. Every so often they speak in a whisper. The graves get older the farther you walk. You can tell because the lettering has worn off some and others are cracked or have fallen over. Soon, the graves are just stones with names written on them, "Killer," "Eustace, treasured fish" and "Here lies Crinkles, beloved cat."

Astrid, Fang, and Alley Cat disappear behind a cluster of saplings and you follow, at a safe distance. The small trees part to reveal a dilapidated cabin. The cabin looks like it is on the brink of collapsing. The only thing that is keeping it together is the black tree growing out of its center.

One by one, they enter the cabin and shut the door.

Turn to the next page.

56

You creep up to the cabin and watch through one of the broken windows. The moon shines through the branches of the black tree. You finally see what Fang and Alley Cat look like. Alley Cat has long red hair and black lipstick on and Fang is a younger blonde girl with braces and very large canine teeth. The girls prepare for Trick Night.

They pick up the floorboards and pull out their store of toilet paper—almost 200 rolls! Once they have organized it into a fort, they sit inside. You shift your position so you can see into the fort. Astrid draws a triangle with chalk on the floor and lights a bundle of sage. Each girl holds a flashlight up to her face and smiles.

"I call this meeting of the Deadly Nightshades to order!" Astrid says. "First order of business: Trick Night! This year we're going to do it a little differently. Instead of TP-ing the outside of the house, we're going to TP the inside!" The Deadly Nightshades look shocked but they agree to go along with the plan. "We'll show the seniors how the Deadly Nightshades do Trick Night," she says. "Let's begin the ceremony."

Go on to the next page.

"Astrid, how are we getting into the house?" Fang asks. Astrid smiles.

"We are going to use a conduit. That way no one will be the wiser. We are going to possess the new neighbors to TP their house for us!"

Fang and Alley Cat gasp. Astrid redraws the triangle in red chalk and whispers a chant as she places a stone on each corner of the triangle.

"Hear us Prudence Deadly, we want to make contact. We want one night to do our mischief right! Heed our call, remember us, the Deadly Nightshades you can trust!" Then Astrid pulls a frog out of her cloak and places it in the middle of the triangle. She then takes three items that were in your backpack: your mother's locket, your dad's handkerchief, and your camera.

"Where did you get all that stuff?" Alley Cat asks.

"It was easy. I just switched backpacks with her," Astrid answers.

She lights a bundle of sage and all three of the girls join hands and hum. Astrid starts the ritual.

If you decide to let her finish the ceremony, turn to page 53.

If you decide to stop the ceremony, turn to page 58.

58

You burst through the door and onto the triangle. The Deadly Nightshades scatter. "Stop the ritual!" you yell.

"Who is that?" Fang asks nervously.

"Is that my new neighbor?" Astrid asks.

"Yes. You're pretty easy to find and follow," you say.

"And you're pretty crafty," Astrid replies. "Do you want to join us?"

You don't know what to say.

"We were deciding what to do next. Every Trick Night we try to make contact with Prudence Deadly," Astrid says.

"What about possessing my family and TP-ing our house?" you ask accusingly.

"Well to be honest, it doesn't work. Really, we've never made contact with Prudence Deadly or possessed anyone. It's just for fun," Alley Cat says. "Supposedly, Prudence Deadly hid her most precious possessions in your basement for hundreds of years!"

"Really?" you say. "So it's a treasure hunt then?"

"We were going to try and make contact with the Ouija board. Do you want to help?" Astrid asks.

If you decide not to trust them, go on to the next page.

If you decide to join them, turn to page 60.

"You can't fool me!" you say and start trashing the cabin. You throw toilet paper everywhere. By the time you are finished, every inch of the cabin—including the Deadly Nightshades—are blanketed in toilet paper. You walk out of the cabin thinking you've got the best of them, or have you? When you get home you find that your house is also covered in toilet paper. Trick Night threw you for a loop!

What will be next?

The End

"Sure. I'll help," you say.

Astrid pulls out a Ouija board and dusts it off. You and the Deadly Nightshades gather around it. She places the planchett on the board and everyone puts their hands on it. You clear your throat and get ready to speak. Little do the Deadly Nightshades know, you've been using Ouija boards since before you could read.

"We pray for our safe journey and communion with any spirits from the other side," Astrid whispers. "We are trying to contact the spirit of Prudence Deadly, leader of the Emerald Coven. Prudence Deadly, if you would like to communicate please let us know." The planchett does not move.

Go on to the next page.

"Please give us a sign," you whisper. The planchett does not move but you hear branches break outside. The four of you sit quietly for a moment and then you hear something scratching on a headstone outside.

"Did you guys hear that?" you ask. They shake their heads. You hear the scratching again but this time it is right behind you.

"Let me try," you say. You begin humming an old lullaby your mom used to sing to you. Then you say: "Prudence Deadly, we're calling you, give us a sign and let us through." The wind picks up and whips through the cabin.

"She's never there," Astrid sighs. Fang sneezes and breaks the circle to grab some toilet paper from the fort.

"No, don't break the circle!" you command as she takes her hands off the planchett. As soon as she does, the planchett begins to spin. You put your hands on it to stop it from flying across the cabin and as soon as you touch it you have three visions.

Your first vision begins with you looking into a mirror. A witch wearing a green cape materializes in front of you. She has bright red hair and black vacant eyes. Her hands come out of the mirror and grab your face.

"Hello, little witch!" says Prudence Deadly. You scream and she disappears.

Turn to the next page.

62

Your second vision is of your old house on the night your neighbors ran you out of town. You are standing in front of your burning house but instead of neighbors, twelve hooded figures gather to watch it burn.

The third is of you sleeping in your new bedroom with lizards covering your bed and the floor! This is like a bad dream. You're back to the mirror and you yell as you rip Prudence Deadly's hands off your head and she disappears cackling. Bang! You're back in the cabin.

"Hey, quit moving the planchett," says Astrid. "We won't be able to make contact, especially after Fang broke the circle."

"But we did make contact! I saw her," you say, "I saw Prudence Deadly! She's in my house."

"You had a vision?!" Alley Cat exclaims. She seems slightly jealous. "But we've been trying to make contact forever." She pauses. "You *are* a Deadly Nightshade." The idea of doing séances and ghost hunting in your new town is exciting but you can't think about that right now.

"That vision was a warning. I have to go home," you say and grab your flashlight.

"Wait, can we come?" Astrid asks.

If you decide to bring the Deadly Nightshades with you, turn to page 65.

If you decide to go home alone, turn to page 118.

There is a tiny door behind the oven. You run to it and dash in before the ceiling sweeps up the rest of the house. You crawl through a damp stone tunnel toward a faint light. It is as if you're in an air duct. A long ladder is set against the edge of the tunnel. You climb down the ladder and find yourself in a dark, foggy hallway.

You squint at the darkness ahead and see doors on either side of the hallway. Each door is outlined with a different glowing color. To your left there is a green door and to your right, a blue door.

You feel instinctively that what's behind one door is completely safe and what's behind the other is fatal. You press your face up to the green door. There are vines growing out of the cracks, and their leaves tickle your face.

You turn toward the blue door and peek through the keyhole. You don't see anything but a thick blue mist and a small figure moving to and fro in the room. She has paws, a white tail and little ears. You look down the hallway. Maybe there are more doors to peek through.

If you decide to go into the green room, turn to page 91.

If you decide to go into the blue room, turn to page 96.

If you decide to walk farther down the hall, turn to page 102.

"Sure you can come," you say. Astrid leads the way. The four of you dash through the cemetery and down the street to your house. As soon as you turn the corner you sprint ahead of the group. You are relieved to see that your house is not on fire and take a second to rest.

"Whew! You're fast!" Fang says.

"What did you see in the vision? Any specific rooms?" Astrid asks. Alley Cat pants behind you.

"What about the basement?" she puffs.

For some reason, the basement feels like the right place to start. You don't have your keys because you snuck out, but Astrid knows a way in. The four of you sneak around the house to your backyard.

"Check this out," Astrid says and she reaches into the broken mouth of one of the largest statues that litters the yard and pulls out a key on a long green velvet ribbon. She walks to the side of your house and pushes some of the ivy away to reveal a keyhole! She pushes the key in and the bricks move to form a door. The four of you slowly duck into the basement.

Turn to the next page.

66

"It's so dusty in here," Fang whispers. You scan the basement with the flashlight and see thousands of boxes stacked to the ceiling. You and Astrid clear a space on the floor and set up the Ouija board.

"Let's try to make contact again," Astrid says. Everyone sits cross-legged and places their hands on the planchett. The Deadly Nightshades begin to hum. You join in and it feels like the most natural thing in the world.

"We are calling on the spirit of Prudence Deadly. Prudence Deadly is there anything you want to show or tell us? We are listening," you say.

"Wait! Can I ask something?" Fang says.

"Sure," you say.

"Do I eat spiders in my sleep?" Fang asks. The planchett moves to "YES" and Fang shudders. "Gross," she says.

"Who moved it?" you ask but everyone shakes their head. "Are you here, Prudence?" you ask. The planchett moves immediately to "YES." "Where?" you ask. The planchett spells out: "UNDER YOU."

Go on to the next page.

You keep holding hands and kick away some of the dust on the floor. The floor cracks and breaks away. You kick harder and under a layer of plaster you find the handle to a trap door.

"I'm breaking the circle!" you announce. The Deadly Nightshades chip away the rest of the floor until they expose the door completely. You knock on it and the knock echoes deeply into the ground.

Alley Cat, Fang, and Astrid pounce on the trap door and pull it up together with a creak. You see the beginning of a staircase, but nothing below the first few steps, even when you shine your flashlight in. It is as if the darkness is feeding on the light.

"It must be Prudence Deadly's secret room!" Alley Cat and Astrid squeal.

"It's so dark down there," Fang whispers.

"Who's first?" you ask but no one volunteers. Then Astrid steps forward.

"I'll do it!" she says, and grabs the flashlight. Halfway down the stairs you hear an ear-splitting crack and the staircase collapses under you. Everyone falls forward.

Turn to the next page.

"Ahhhhrgh!" you yell as you land on the stone floor with a thump. Alley Cat and Fang land on you with a thud.

"Is everyone all right?" you groan and try to move your arms and legs to make sure nothing is broken.

"I'm okay," Astrid calls back. You get up and steady yourself against the wall. Fang and Alley Cat are helping each other out of the rubble.

"Does the flashlight still work?" you ask. Astrid shakes it to produce a faint beam of light. She spies a torch in the room. Astrid fishes in her pocket for her matches and lights the torch. The room is bathed in a warm glow. She points the flame up the unusable staircase. It's a ten-foot drop. Now there is no way out. The torch illuminates a long dark hallway in front of you.

"Only one way to go now," you say. You grab another torch and light it with Astrid's. The four of you enter the corridor. At the entrance you feel something against your ankles.

"Wait, I think it's booby-trapped," you say, and toss a piece of stairwell onto the wire. Immediately a trap door to another pit opens in the floor.

Go on to the next page.

"Watch out for the stones and walls," you announce. You can hear something very large breathing in the hole. "This is no ordinary hall." Suddenly, Alley Cat trips and hits the wall. The wall moves under her hands and opens, releasing hundreds of bats into the corridor!

You wave your torch to keep the bats at bay. You turn off the corridor and lose the bats. You are in a small, very dusty room off the hallway.

"That was something!" Astrid says. Fang explores the room and Alley Cat takes a rest.

"I don't think bats are as bad as spiders," Fang says. It is then that you realize something about the dust lining the walls of the room: it's hanging in large sacks, like eggs, from the ceiling. You hear the same heavy breathing you heard from the first trap. You raise your torch and see a huge green spider hanging over Fang!

"It's just that spiders have so many legs," she says, and leans on part of the web. "Ew. It's sticky!"

"Fang...move away from that web," you whisper. Fang turns around and before she can scream the spider has her.

If you decide to save Fang, turn to page 72.

If you decide to run, turn to page 123.

Something does not feel right about all this. You decide to give Peter's supply closet a pass.

"Thanks but I've got to go," you say. You dash down the hallway, almost slipping on the floor as you turn the corner and *bang!* you slam into Astrid.

"Ouch!" says Astrid. "Watch it!"

"Sorry, the janitor—he tried to—he invited me into his closet," you say breathlessly.

"What?! You've got to stay away from him." Astrid looks around. "Nobody goes near that closet, ever. People say he used to kidnap students and use their hair for mops. We've got to hide!" she whispers, and the two of you sneak into an open classroom. Eventually, the coast is clear.

"Do you know why he doesn't speak?" you ask.

"I heard someone cut his tongue out in prison," she says and smiles. "Don't you believe me about the mops made of human hair?" she asks. "I can get you proof."

If you decide to ask Astrid for proof of hair mops, turn to page 76.

If you believe what Astrid says, turn to page 84.

72

"We have to save her!" you cry. The only weapon you have is your torch and it will have to do.

"HELP!!" Fang manages to scream before the mother spider wraps her head in the web.

"Light the egg sacks on fire," you order. You and Astrid hurry, lighting all the egg sacks. The mother spider charges you, her red eyes looking directly into yours. Meanwhile, Alley Cat rips Fang out of her cocoon and they escape. You grab a ball of web, light it on fire, and hurl it at the mother spider. It shatters against her face, blinding her permanently.

At the end of the hallway there is a green door, and the four of you push through and slam it behind you. Astrid lights another torch on the wall. You find yourself in a small stone room with a table and green velvet curtains. Four velvet robes hang in the corner and a big book sits on the table. There is also a cabinet filled with curious jars and vials of unidentifiable creatures and plants.

"Is everyone all right?" Alley Cat asks. Fang murmurs something about feeling dizzy and you look around for something to give her.

Go on to the next page.

"This is it! This is Prudence Deadly's room," Astrid says. You gather together and pick Fang up and put her on the table. You wrap her in one of the velvet cloaks.

"We should be safe from spiders in here," Alley Cat says soothingly.

"Wow, look at this," Astrid says, picking up a huge leather-bound book. She grows silent as she leafs through its pages. "This is Prudence Deadly's diary," she whispers.

Astrid brings over the diary and places it on the table. She reads the first page out loud: "'Property of Prudence Deadly, age 13.' That's our age!" The diary is filled with detailed entries about her early life, and it even said a few things about her sister Zora Belladonna.

"I didn't know she had a sister," Astrid says. The diary also includes numerous creature-summoning spells and deadly potion recipes.

Fang stops sweating and sits up, looking at all the curious vials in the room. Taking a cue from her improved state, you ask, "shall we have a reading?"

To keep exploring the ritual room,
turn to page 113.

To read Prudence Deadly's diary,
turn to page 122.

74

You decide to set up some traps for the Deadly Nightshades first. The red-haired ghost can wait. From watching your parents, you know that gathering evidence of a break-in is very similar to finding evidence of spirits.

First, you rig some motion sensor cameras to flash on the main stairway and down the hall. You also rig a spring that releases fake ghosts when the basement door opens. Then you place a bucket of feathers and syrup above the front door so that it falls when an intruder steps on a string of fishing line. (You hope your parents do not set anything off.)

You go into the kitchen to make a celebratory sandwich. As you are spreading mayonnaise on some bread, you see a flash from upstairs. You drop the sandwich and run.

You gasp when you reach the top and see a young girl in a Victorian dress facing away from you. She rips open the letters from Astrid's backpack, reading some, and then throwing them over her shoulder. The girl starts humming to herself and rocking back and forth. She has not seen you.

*If you decide to sneak up on her,
turn to page 110.*

*If you decide to wake up your parents and trap
her, turn to page 112.*

I bet I scared them off! you think. You blow the candle out and pull the blanket over your head. Shadows dance across your bedroom walls. You drift off and immediately start to dream.

You are standing in the living room of your old house at night, and for a moment everything looks normal. You walk around the house remembering all the good times you had in each room and then everything changes. The rooms begin to shrink. It starts with the rug and then the walls start to crack and curve in. The shrinking starts slowly and quickens the more you try to escape.

You squeeze through the narrowing hallways and run down the stairs. The house is swallowing itself and if you are not careful it's going to swallow you up too. The doors and windows are disappearing, and soon there will be no escape!

You run from room to room watching your house and the memories in it contract into darkness. You dash into the kitchen and dodge clattering plates and shattering windows. You dive under the table but it immediately shrinks and balances on your back. Then you notice something you've never seen before.

Turn to page 63.

"I don't believe you, Astrid. Peter cleans school floors with mops made of hair?" you challenge.

"Follow me," Astrid replies.

She peeks around the corner and motions for you to follow. You scamper back up the hallway to Peter's closet. First Astrid presses herself against the wall and jiggles the closet doorknob. It's locked. Then she pulls a bobby pin out of her hair and picks the lock until you hear a click. Astrid pushes on the door and it opens.

"We're in!" she says. "Are you coming?"

"I'm not sure," you say.

"If the mop rumor is true then we'll find the hair mops in this closet," she says. If we get any dirt on him he'll be gone for good." Astrid grabs your arm. "We could be the ones who finally expose him. We would be the toast of the school!" Astrid exclaims.

If you decide to follow Astrid into the closet, turn to page 37.

If you decide to run away, turn to page 108.

The best choice is to alert the authorities, you think. You tell your parents about the walkie-talkie and they spring into action. Your dad calls 9-1-1 and speaks to the operator. Within five minutes there is an authoritative knock on the door.

"That was fast!" your dad mumbles and opens the door. A small, round police officer stands in the doorway. You stifle a laugh.

"Evening folks, I'm Officer Treacle. We got a call about a neighborhood disturbance," Officer Treacle says in a surprisingly deep voice. You tell him about the threat of TP-ing the house.

"Not a huge surprise there," he says. "We used to get calls from this house all the time, especially this time of year. 'Trick Night' is one of our busiest times of the year. All these kids getting a jump on Halloween by pranking their neighbors," Officer Treacle mutters. "The way I see it there are two ways to do this. We can walk around the house and secure it or we can take a look at the evidence."

If you decide to secure the house,
turn to page 17.

If you decide to show him the backpack,
turn to page 18.

You hit the dirty water. In an instant it dissolves into a brilliant flash of blue light. Then you are twisting and turning through a tunnel of light. You are flying through time and space!

"WHAT'S HAPPENING???" you scream. You hear the honk of taxis dissolving into the clip-clop of horses' hooves. You land with a PLUNK! and find yourself underground in a vast crypt lit by torches. Peter is sitting in the corner rocking back and forth. The walls are covered in mossy skulls and bones. Clusters of rectangular marble tombs cover the huge catacomb.

"Are we at the Metropolitan Museum?" you ask. Peter nods. You grab a torch made from a tibia and turn to him.

"What now?" you ask, but he just hides his face and points over your shoulder to a grave in the corner of the room. "Over there?" you ask. Peter nods without looking up.

Unlike the tombs, this is a solitary grave dug into the earth. The headstone has a huge stone lizard sitting on top of it. You shudder as you draw closer. It feels like the lizard is watching you. You stare into Prudence Deadly's grave.

Turn to page 80.

80

Instead of a plot of dirt, the gravesite is unfilled. Inside there is a simple wooden coffin. The top of the coffin is slightly askew. You bring the torch closer to the coffin and read the lid out loud: "Here lies Prudence Deadly."

You feel a cool breeze whip through the catacombs. You look behind you and see a cloaked figure watching you. The wind gets stronger and then you hear a deafening *crack!* The bones that make up the walls are starting to break. The gusts of wind are loosening them. You take shelter in the grave as the wind blows harder and the lizard begins to glow above you.

"It's empty!" you yell and Peter nods. Suddenly the coffin begins to sink and you smell mop water. Peter touches the glowing lizard and the light moves through his body, lighting his insides. Peter does not look afraid.

"What's happening?" you ask and Peter grabs your hand and brings it toward the carved lizard's face. It radiates heat.

*If you decide to touch the lizard statue,
turn to page 98.*

*If you want to get out of the grave now,
turn to page 107.*

You decide to search the basement. You creep through the living room and duck under the stairs. You grab one of the packed flashlights and climb into the dumbwaiter.

If anyone is down there I'll have the element of surprise on my side, you think to yourself. You unlock the dumbwaiter and pull up the door. You plug your nose to keep the stench of old food out. You leave the door open and lower yourself down into the basement.

You flip on the flashlight and leap out of the dumbwaiter. Crash! You land heavily on some old boxes and all manner of plates and silverware spills out of them making an enormous commotion.

So much for being quiet, you think and slide down the boxes. You eventually move enough boxes out of the way to reach the light in the middle of the room. You pull on the chain and the basement is filled with an ancient yellow light. You scan the basement but you don't see anyone. Then Teacup pokes her head over the edge of the stairs.

"So you're the culprit!" you say, laughing. Then you spot something that makes you stop.

Turn to the next page.

Some of the boxes you knocked down have exposed a tiny door in the wall, painted with triangles and a big green lizard. You take a deep breath and turn the knob. It doesn't budge. You look around for something to pry it open with. Teacup is standing on an antique iron with a sharp edge. She hisses as you grab it from under her paws.

Screech! The door opens and sand pours out from the other side. You jump back and search through the sand. When you scan the area with your flashlight, you spy a black doctor's bag. You reach in and grab it.

You pull out the bag and dust it off. You unsnap the bag and reach inside and feel around. You feel the spine of a book. You pour the bag out and sift through the contents. You find an old moth-eaten cloak, a small book, and a white mask with green lips.

You turn the mask over in your hands and are about to put it on when you hear a noise behind you. A rat scampers by you. You turn back to the book and open to the first page. It reads: "Property of Prudence Deadly, age 13. KEEP OUT."

If you decide to continue reading, turn to page 86.

If you decide to put on the mask, turn to page 116.

Astrid sounds pretty convincing and you decide to trust her. Wrong choice! Astrid is a descendant of Prudence Deadly and part of an extended network of the Emerald Coven called the Deadly Nightshades. Little did you know that *Murdoch's Myths* was the giveaway. When she saw you with it, she knew that you knew too much.

As the leader of the Emerald Coven, Astrid has a duty to get rid of you. She whispers a short but fatal spell, and disappears. You try to leave but your feet are cemented to the tile floor. You try to scream but no sound comes out. Grimy black ash begins to float down from the ceiling, sizzling as it hits your skin. Flake by flake, you burn to death, your own ashes indistinct from the rest.

You are trapped forever and forced to roam the halls of your school. You try to warn other students about Astrid, but unlike you, they do not listen to ghosts!

The End

You see another spell called: "Beginner's Conjuring." It calls for a picture of the one you want summoned and the repetition of the phrase "little ghost, little ghost, come be my host." You don the black cape and put the mask next to the book. You turn to the picture of Prudence Deadly. You find some big candles in a box and light them. You arrange them in a circle and sit in the middle with the book in front of you.

You chant the rhyme making sure to get louder and louder. *It probably won't work*, you think. You love to hold séances and try to conjure spirits. It is exciting to find a new spell.

Your mouth starts to feel very dry. You begin to cough and a white powder drifts out of your mouth like smoke. You start to cough so hard that you accidentally swallow some of the powder.

"I summon Prudence Deadly," you sputter. A green mist forms around you and when it clears Astrid is sitting in the circle with you.

"Astrid?! Are you Prudence?"

She shakes her head no.

If you decide to believe Astrid,
turn to page 120.

If you decide to question her, turn to page 121.

86

You keep looking through the diary. The next page is a black and white photo of a young Prudence Deadly looking very solemn in a black cloak. Prudence holds a gnarled black dinosaur claw with long nails. Under the photo in script a caption reads:

Last known evidence of the sacred relic "Gaia's Claw."

The book is filled with amateur potion studies. There is a very complicated recipe for Cherry Lane pie. It's all about your house. The diary reads:

WARNING: This spell is not for amateurs.
If baked correctly, this pie will vanquish ene-
mies. But if made incorrectly, or not eaten in
its entirety, there will be dire consequences.
This pie will drain the victim of their powers
and bind them to the baker for eternity!

The spell calls for a pound of black cherries, a lizard heart, earth from the back yard of your house, and a drop of blood from the baker. When the victim takes their last bite the baker must say: "Eat your heart out." After the last bite the victim will be bewitched.

If you decide to look at other spells, turn to page 85.

If you decide to read on in hopes you'll learn more about this spell, turn to page 89.

I have never had a dream like that before, you think. You hear another crash, deeper in the house this time. *Now what?* you think to yourself. You get out of bed and creep down the hall. You peek over the balcony but you don't see anything. You tiptoe down the stairs and look into the living room. You still don't see anyone.

In the foyer you see a box of your parents' cameras that has fallen over.

That's it. You pick the cameras up and place them gingerly back in the box. The moonlight in the living room is really beautiful and you decide to take a few shots. You put the camera on a timer and stand by the window. The camera counts down from thirty and you wait patiently. The house is very quiet. The flash goes off and all at once you hear another crash of boxes and then a giggle coming from somewhere. You grab the camera and check out the photo. There is someone standing outside the window behind you, smiling. You hear feet scampering over the floor on the other side of the house. *What is making that noise?* you wonder.

If you decide to search the basement,
turn to page 81.

If you decide to search the kitchen,
turn to page 114.

Prudence Deadly eventually walks over to your cage and taps on the glass. You take cover under a log and another lizard comes out of hiding. You thought you were alone. Prudence flicks her hand and the bars separate like flower petals. The other lizard hops out. She pours a black liquid onto the lizard.

"Please, please don't kill me," the minister whimpers.

"Oh, I'm not going to kill you. I just want you to sing to me, if you would,"

"Sing?" he asks haltingly.

"Yes, SING!" Prudence orders and when the minister opens his mouth the lizard leaps in. Suddenly he is unable to speak. He chokes but no sound comes out. The lizard hops back out but his voice is still gone.

"It will be hard for you to pray for my wicked soul without a voice," Prudence says shrilly. "For the rest of time you, your children, your grandchildren will be mute!" She cackles and puts the lizard back in the cage.

The lizard looks at you and whispers, "Can you hear me?" He sounds just like the minister. "I can get us home if you trust me," he says.

If you decide to go with the minister lizard, turn to page 36.

If you decide to stay where you are in the reptile house, turn to page 109.

You decide to read through the book. Prudence Deadly pasted the photos of the souls she captured all through the book. Her entries become increasingly disjointed and unorganized. On the last page of the book there is a counter-spell to release all the souls. It simply says: "Burn this book."

At that moment, you hear breathing behind you. A giggle follows the breathing. You turn and come face to face with the white mask! You scream and grab the book to defend yourself. Then the intruder raises her mask.

"Gotcha!" Astrid says. "Pretty cool, huh? Scary mask! Where did you get it?"

"Found it in the wall," you say.

"Wow, look at this stuff," Astrid says and dons the black cloak.

"Yeah, it's pretty weird stuff. I guess it belonged to someone who used to live here." At that moment the lights dim. Astrid dances around in the cloak. She grabs the mask and puts it on.

"Let me grab my flashlight," you say and walk across the room to grab the light.

Turn to the next page.

90

You flick the switch on the flashlight but for some reason it doesn't work. Then the basement suddenly goes dark. You shake the flashlight.

"Astrid?" you ask. "Say something! I can't see anything." You switch the batteries around in the flashlight and it starts to flicker.

"Are you close?" you ask. You scan the room with the flickering flashlight but you don't see her. Then you see her standing in the middle of the room holding the diary against her chest. She is sniffling.

"Astrid?" you whisper. A piercing scream fills the basement. Blood pours out of Astrid's mouth and she collapses. You run to her but when you get to her the cloak is empty. Then you feel Astrid's hands around your neck.

"Please, no," you manage to choke out. Astrid attacks as the flashlight rolls out of your hand. You thrash and reach for the flashlight. Your fingers close around the light and you whack Astrid on the head. The light dances and she lets go enough for you to crawl away.

You shine the light at Astrid and she recoils. Scales cover her body and she hisses.

Turn to page 95.

The green door looks more welcoming than the blue. You turn the knob and walk into the jungle room. The room is very humid and even though you strain your eyes to see, you can only just make out your hands in front of your face because of the thick condensation. You touch the walls and they are moist and leafy.

You walk deeper into the jungle room. Your feet crunch on sticks and underbrush. The heat gets heavier and heavier. You jump when you feel claws scuttle over your feet.

It's so hot in here, you think. Slowly a shape starts to materialize, and you find yourself nearing a hut. You can hear someone puttering around and humming. You knock on the door and a very raspy voice tells you to enter.

The hut is filled with chalk drawings of lizards climbing all over the walls and ceiling. A large woman wrapped in a shawl sits on a mat preparing food.

"Come in, we've been waiting for you," she says.

"Who are you?" you ask.

Turn to the next page.

92

"I am your great-great-great-grandmother," she says, and a fat green lizard scuttles up her back.

"I don't remember meeting you," you say timidly.

"Well, that could be because I haven't left this jungle in two hundred years," she chuckles and flicks some meat into her bowl. Your great-great great-grandmother offers you some Cherry Lane pie.

The air feels cooler in the hut. The Cherry Lane pie is very bitter and muddy. You secretly spit it out when your grandmother is not looking.

"How old are you now?" she inquires.

"I just turned thirteen," you say. She smiles to herself and looks at you. There is a green flash in her eyes.

"This is an important year for you. We must celebrate! Please have some more pie," she pushes the pot towards you.

"No thank you, I'm fine," you say. But she fills your plate up anyway and brings it up to your mouth.

"Eat your heart out," she says. You shut your eyes and suddenly you feel lizards all over you. You scream and cover your face.

Then something happens.

Turn to page 94.

Blue light shoots out of your fingers and suddenly the hut is on fire. You look at your great-great-great-grandmother but she has fainted from the smoke. You stand up and try to pull her out of the burning hut but she is heavy.

The hut begins to disappear and suddenly you are standing in an empty white room with your great-great-great-grandmother at your feet. You look around for some way to help her. You turn toward the hallway but she grasps your ankle and squeezes.

"You are more powerful than I thought you'd be for such a young witch," she gasps.

"Let go of me!" you shout. Then you hear footsteps. Her body disintegrates with a hiss, and hundreds of bright green geckos leap out. Cloaked figures fill the room. One of the figures with bright red hair steps forward and extends a thin hand covered in emeralds.

"Join us," says the red-headed figure. The other figures chant the same words and they get louder until you cover your ears. The black cloaks surround you, chanting louder and louder, until you wake up in the dark room, gasping for air.

Turn to page 87.

"Astrid?" you whisper.

"I am not Astrid anymore!" says the creature, hissing through her sharp teeth.

"Who are you?" you ask.

"I am Prudence Deadly and I've come to initiate you. It has been centuries since I've possessed a human. You see, I've been in hiding, but you already knew that didn't you? Any relation to my nemesis Zora Belladonna would be shrewd enough to figure that out. With Zora out of the way we can be powerful together!" Prudence cackles.

Teacup brushes against your leg. In a flash of blue light, Zora Belladonna stands beside you, clad in a white furry robe.

"She is not going anywhere with you if I can help it," Zora purrs. She stands in front of you, ready to fight Prudence off. Then you can hear Zora communicating with you telepathically, "There are two ways to fight her," Zora whispers, "You can use your powers or you can undo the curse on this house!" What should you do next?

If you decide to fight Prudence Deadly with Zora, turn to page 117.

If you decide to undo the curse on your house, turn to page 119.

You turn the knob of the blue door and it opens softly. The room is filled with the same blue mist, but it smells of lavender. It quickly dissipates as you enter. You are standing in a furnished room and all of the surfaces and walls are covered in photos of your family.

You walk around the room admiring the photos and then you start to notice something odd. There is a woman standing in the background of all the pictures. Sometimes she's just a shadow but sometimes she's smiling with her arms around your parents. You look at the most recent picture of you and your parents in front of your old house.

There she is! A smiling shadow sitting next to you. You hear a noise behind you and see Teacup walking to and fro in the room. You pick her up and grab a photo to get a better look, but Teacup struggles and leaps out of your arms. The frame clatters to the ground and Teacup disappears. You pick up the photo and hear someone clear their throat behind you.

Go on to the next page.

You whip around and come face to face with a thin woman with long white hair dressed in a white fur gown.

"Who are you?" you stammer.

"My name is Zora Belladonna and I am your great-great-great-aunt on your father's side," Zora says, and smiles.

"Well, how did you find me?" you ask.

"Oh, I've always been here. I wanted to formally introduce myself. You see, my darling, we can meet here anytime. We are the only witches that know about this place."

"Witches?!" you whisper perplexed.

"Yes, I am a witch and so are you!" Zora's words disappear as you wake up with a jolt. You grab the first photo of your family you see, light a candle, and slump down. It's a fairly old photo of you, your parents, and Teacup beside a lake. You sigh with relief as you see that Zora is not in the photo. Then Teacup in the photo moves, she licks her paws and winks! You scream and throw the photo across the room.

"Zora? Are you here?" Teacup answers with an affirmative purr. At that moment you hear a crash.

Turn to page 87.

98

You let Peter press your hand into the lizard's head. Once again you are spinning in a tube of blue light. You're going further back this time. The Central Park Zoo's ivy-covered exterior looms over you. *Whoosh!* You fly inside, past the seals and penguins, and into the reptile house.

Another flash of blue and you can feel your body twisting and changing shape, but it is not painful. You can feel your arms getting shorter and your skin sprouting scales. All you can hear is your heavy breathing resounding against the walls. That's when you realize that you are in a cage. You open your mouth to scream, but all that comes out is a hiss.

Somehow you've traveled back in time and into the body of a lizard! You press your scaly face against the gate. You look up. It's Prudence Deadly in the flesh. She wears an emerald robe with red hair cascading down her back. She is so glamorous, but her eyes hold a dark truth.

Prudence drags a woman with long black hair and a blue cloak and places her near the rattle snake cage. The snakes wrap around her wrists. Next to her there is a minister. He looks just like Peter.

Go on to the next page.

The minister appears bound to obey Prudence. They appear to be performing an exorcism on Zora. "This is your last chance, Zora!" Prudence says. "Tell me where Gaia's Claw is."

The minister who looks like Peter speaks. "We will pray for your lost soul Zora, you wicked witch!"

"It is in safe hands," Zora whispers.

"I refuse to live in the body of a caged creature for another day," Prudence seethes.

"Then come home to your family," says Zora.

Prudence cackles, "You are no sister of mine! I hope our parents perish in the tomb I imprisoned them in."

"I freed them myself," Zora says.

"You rat!" Prudence turns on her. "Gaia's Claw was passed down to me." She bursts into tears, "You were always the favorite child!" Prudence takes a deep breath. "'Oh, Zora is so kind' they would say. 'Zora plays with the other witches and doesn't spend all day digging in the woods.'" Prudence raises her hands and green light shoots out of her fingertips straight into Zora's chest. When your eyes adjust Zora is unconscious and her hair is white.

Turn to the next page.

"What have you done?" the minister whispers.

"My parents did not understand, and that's why I had to lock them up. And I will destroy you if you stand in my way," Prudence hisses. She gives the priest a wild look and her green eyes flash.

Now the story is clear. The rift between Zora and Prudence was borne out of sibling rivalry. Prudence claimed her work was for good, but she really just wanted control of the plants and animals for herself. When the claw was stolen, the Emerald Coven had to hide out in the bodies of the reptiles in the Central Park Zoo until they could retrieve it and gain their power back.

But even before that, the sisters were from different worlds. Zora was from a world that brought creatures together. Prudence was from a lonely world of darkness. She believed the Emerald Coven was her true family and would do anything to protect them.

"Now where is that claw?" Prudence asks.

You watch helplessly as Prudence Deadly continues to torture the minister. His screams echo through the reptile house.

Turn to page 88.

102

You want to explore the whole hallway. Who knows what could be in the other rooms? You pass by so many doors; you think there are no colors left until a deep red door appears in the darkness. You arrive at the door and grasp the doorknob.

"Ouch!" you yelp. The doorknob is so hot it is almost untouchable. You turn around but the other doors have disappeared. The red door is your only choice now.

You take a deep breath and twist the knob quickly. As soon as you turn the knob you feel yourself being pulled through the door and into the room. Then everything starts to spin and you land on your stomach under your parents' bed.

You hear your parents murmuring about something above you. You slide to the edge of the bed and stick your ear out. At first you think it is nothing but then you catch something your mom says that makes your ears perk up.

"Our Rabbit isn't old enough to know the truth. Thirteen is still too young," your mom insists.

"We've got to come clean soon about the women in my family or it will just get too complicated," your dad argues.

Go on to the next page.

"But I've never seen any of the signs Zora was talking about," your mom argues.

"Zora said the powers start manifesting themselves as dreams. You can leave your body in spirit and travel anywhere you want," he says. "The powers become active at the age of thirteen but the catch is that every witch is different. You develop your powers when you're ready," he says.

"So if we hear of any strange dreams, we have the 'you might be a witch' conversation?" your mom asks.

Am I still dreaming? you wonder. After your parents turn off the light you sneak down the hallway and into your room. Your house is filled with a thick haze. You press your hands onto your comforter and feel tiny feet rush over your hands. You strike a match and open your canopy.

What you see cannot be explained. Instead of an empty bed you see yourself sleeping peacefully. You gasp for breath and drop the match. It catches the canopy and the whole bed goes up in flames instantly.

Turn to the next page

104

"Wake up! Wake up!" you scream at yourself but to no avail. You can hear shouting from outside as the fire moves through the house. For a moment, you think you are reliving the last night you had in your old home. But then you come to a startling realization.

It's happening again and it's all my fault, you think. *I've been starting fires in my dreams! I must be a witch!* You can feel the flames lapping at your face and eyelashes.

Without really thinking about it you open your mouth and blow. The flames rise high for a moment, but, like birthday candles, your breath extinguishes them. You smile; maybe you could get a handle on this witch thing. You wake up to Teacup licking your face. You are yourself again, and Teacup purrs softly next to you.

You lie back and relax for a moment. Could that dream have any truth to it? Are you really a witch? You make a mental note to talk to your parents in the morning. You are about to drift back to sleep when you hear a crash downstairs.

Turn to page 87.

You do not want to miss your first lunch at a new school. You jump up and gather your things. You put *Murdoch's Myths* in your bag and head for the exit. You turn the knob but it's locked! You knock on the door and jiggle the knob but to no avail.

"Hey! I'm locked in!" you say and bang on the door as hard as you can. The librarian appears in the doorway grinning. You wave and signal that you're locked in. She taps her green nails on the door and pulls out the key on a velvet ribbon. You motion excitedly to the key and then, to your horror, you watch the librarian swallow the key whole.

She runs her thumb across her throat and cackles. Then you hear a loud creaking behind you and turn to see a huge bookshelf falling toward you. The last thing you see before you are crushed to death is the librarian's gleaming green eyes.

The End

106

You try to open the door to the main library, but it won't budge. There is a big window over one of the shelves and you climb up and bang against it. You can see the rest of your classmates eating lunch outside as if nothing is happening. You yell louder but no one can hear you. You press yourself against the window but the flames rise quickly. You begin to cough and choke. In a short while, you stop breathing altogether.

At the end of the school day, the librarian checks the stacks. She finds you curled up in the back of the room clutching the smoking card with Peter's code on it. You have fallen victim to the curse of Cherry Tree Lane.

The End

You start to climb out of Prudence Deadly's grave but the mud is like quicksand and sucks you back in. You land in the coffin with a bang. The earth bubbles underneath you and pops like lava. You feel the hard, splintered back of the empty coffin and you reach up to find something to grab onto. The solid top of the coffin tumbles down and hits your head. You push at it. You've got to get out. But it doesn't budge.

Then to your horror you hear the slow, even thud of the nails being driven in.

The End

You turn around and push Astrid away.

"Leave me alone," you say. You push her too hard and she slips on the wet floor. Astrid stumbles down the hallway and steps back onto the stairs. She falls for about two stories. By the time the paramedics arrive, she's dead.

You are charged with manslaughter and sentenced to life under house arrest. You soon realize that the house on Cherry Tree Lane is much worse than any prison.

The End

This is all too much. What if it is a trick and Prudence Deadly is trying to capture you?

"We have to go now, while the cage is open!" he says.

"No," you say, and cross your scaly claws. "How can I trust you?"

The other lizard leaps out of your cage and tries to escape through a drain pipe. But Prudence catches him and with a wave of her hand exiles him from the human world.

The spell also extends to you. You live out the rest of your days as a scaly, bewitched lizard, being ogled by horrible children eating candy and banging on the glass.

The End

110

You creep up to the young girl. She continues to open letters with her back turned. You are about to touch her shoulder when she spins around and faces you. Her face is still young and very pale. She looks at you with a suspicious look.

"I see you!" she screams and begins to levitate slightly so you have to look up at her. Then she squints her eyes and starts to cry, but instead of tears a thick green liquid oozes out of her eyes.

"No letters from him in weeks!" she says. Then she bursts into tears and covers you in thick slime. The ghost flies down the hall sobbing.

"Wait!" you say and run after her. You slip on the green slime and slam into the table and fall, and the ghost stops in front of a window at the end of the hallway. You rub your knee and rev up to catch her. "Wait! I want to talk!" you cry and dive toward her. Next thing you know you're sailing through her and out the open window.

The End

"Mom! Dad!" you scream. "I saw one!" Your parents wake up and come running.

"Are you all right?" your mom asks, feeling your head.

"What happened? Why is everyone up?" your dad asks.

"I found real evidence!" you say. "There was a full ghost in the hallway!"

The three of you review the last ten minutes of footage from the motion detector camera. The tape is just static except for a ten second sequence.

What you see is shocking. You see yourself running through the hallway surrounded by hundreds of ghosts. They scream silently and rip at your clothes and hair. Your dad turns the sound up and suddenly a high-pitched wail fills the house. Your dad takes the tape out of the machine and it has the words "GET OUT" scratched on the outside.

You move again, this time to an apartment in the heart of New York City, but not for long. The footage makes you and your parents famous, and you are called on to hunt demons all over the world!

The End

You and the Deadly Nightshades walk around the ritual room looking at everything. There are strange creatures in jars and menacing Venus fly-traps, some with human teeth!

You look at a vial of white powder that has a green "XXX" on it. You are about to open it when Fang bumps you and the whole vial spills on the floor. Before you can say anything the powder jumps down everyone's throats and you are trapped in the ritual room forever.

The End

"That crash came from the kitchen," you say to yourself. You walk into the kitchen and gasp. It's a disaster! All the windows are open and it is freezing. At least two-dozen cats scatter like shadows as you enter. There are cats on the table, the chairs, and all over the cupboards. Broken plates and food are everywhere. They must have gotten into the refrigerator. You grab a broom and try to usher them out the windows.

Your mom comes in and laughs when she sees you ushering cats out of the kitchen with a broom.

"I guess Teacup was having a milk mixer," she says and grabs a pail and a mop. After cleaning for a while, you and your mom make some warm milk for yourselves.

You drink in silence until your mom says, "Now that you are 13, I'd like to tell you a little bit about your family history." Your mom takes a breath and then continues, "You come from a very talented family of witches!"

The End

116

You turn the mask over and brush it off. You brush against something warm and alive, and feel a tiny mouth around your thumb in response.

"Ouch!" you yell, and put your wounded thumb in your mouth, tasting blood. A tiny lizard crawls out of the mask's mouth hole, hisses at you, and scuttles across the floor. *Gross,* you think, and look back at the mask. A little bit of your blood from your thumb drips around the mouth where the lizard appeared. Suddenly the mask begins to shake. The basement lights go out. The mask soars out of your hands and levitates above you, casting an eerie green glow.

A monster begins to grow out of the mask. It is another lizard. This one is at least ten times bigger than the one that bit you. The mask remains on the lizard's face, white against the electric green glow of its scaly body. The lizard continues to grow and slithers toward you slowly. Then it strikes. Biting your legs with its electric teeth, it pulls you into the hole in the wall. The last thing you see is the wall growing back, cutting off the light. You are trapped in the darkness. Two weeks later the police excavate the basement. The police and your parents finally find your body covered in green hissing lizards.

The End

You decide to fight Prudence Deadly with Zora.

"Let's settle the score, Zora!" Prudence commands, her snake tongue lapping at the air. She raises her long fingers and they transform into snakes that attack you, spitting venom everywhere. Zora pulls you out of the way but a little bit of the venom hits your hand.

You wince. Now you are really mad. Zora looks into your eyes and grabs your burned hand. Her hand feels cool and it does not hurt. The two of you are connected.

"Oh Prudence. Don't you know that blood is thicker than venom?" Zora yells. An orb of blue light appears in front of you and grows brighter the tighter you hold Zora's hand.

"Two witches are better than one!" you both scream, and the words send the blue light flying into Prudence Deadly. You hear a crash and the basement starts to crumble. Geysers of green light shoot out of the ground. You and Zora step back. Prudence runs this way and that, trying to dodge the light.

At that moment, the wall cracks open and she tries to make her escape. But just as she nears the hole, two green claws pull Prudence Deadly down into the depths of the Earth.

The End

118

"I have to go home by myself," you say to the Deadly Nightshades. You run out of the cabin, knocking over some of the toilet paper fort and almost tripping over the broken cabin steps. You sprint in the direction of your house, your nightmare hot on your mind. Suddenly you stop. Didn't you just pass this tombstone with the carved angel?

Lightning strikes overhead and rain begins to pelt your face. You know something is very wrong. Your vision was clear. It's happening again. You finally find your way out of Lockworm Cemetary and run the rest of the way home. But it's no use. By the time you get to your house, the unimaginable has already happened. You arrive home to a charred skeleton of your new house. Your parents are nowhere to be seen.

The End

You realize what she means by curse. Of course! The book of captured souls.

"Zora! I need a flame," you say. You take the book with all the photos of captured souls out of your cloak. Zora snaps her fingers and produces a blue flame. You hold the book over the flame and it burns up instantly. The room is filled with a pale blue light.

"Is anyone here?" you ask nervously. You slap your flashlight and the light flashes.

"We are here," a strange voice says. The flashlight finally works and families surround you.

"Our souls were trapped in this house but now you've released us," one of the ghosts says.

"Thank you," they murmur, and the basement resounds with praise. Then, one by one, they float up, through the ceiling and into the Harvest moon.

It is the most beautiful thing you have ever seen.

The End

120

You almost believe Astrid.

"But I summoned Prudence!" you say, not quite understanding her. "And you came. It must have worked."

Astrid's eyes flash and then fade. She smiles, but her teeth rot in front of your face, and lizards crawl out of her mouth and eye sockets. Astrid is decomposing in front of you. Her body lunges toward you. She tries to clasp you to her chest, but you push her off. You keep pushing until Astrid is no more.

A few hours later your parents find you in your basement covered in Astrid's blood and muttering about witches and lizards.

They are forced to commit you to an asylum.

The End

You pause.

"But it must have worked," you say nervously. Astrid nods and smiles. She dons her black cloak and mask and does a little spin in the room.

"It certainly feels good to have a human body again," she says. "This one is so young I will get a lot of wear out of it."

She begins to dance hypnotically around the basement. Her body resembles a snake in the way she dips and twists from side to side. You are entranced. "If you released me I must give you something in return," she says.

You hear yourself say something in a monotone voice, a voice that is not yours. "I want to be like you, I want unlimited power," you say.

"Unlimited power?" she cackles. "What about a nice tail or rattles on the ends of your toes?" she asks.

"I want to be like you, you are all-powerful," you say. Prudence smiles.

"You are so kind to say that!" she says, and puts her cold hand on your head. She whispers a few indistinct words. You feel yourself shrinking, sprouting wings and tiny legs. You have been transformed into a cockroach.

"Now you can be my apprentice," says Prudence Deadly.

The End

You spread the diary out on the table and look through the pages. You find a chapter dedicated to Prudence Deadly's pets. Unfortunately you are quite familiar with these pets. They are the huge spiders that you just escaped from.

Her spiders are descendents of ancient Arachnids that were thought to have been extinct. Prudence conjured the spirits of the extinct spiders into live spiders. The spirit would transform the host, eventually growing to the size you saw.

The problem with having big pets is that they have huge appetites. These spiders could eat only souls and to keep them healthy Prudence had to feed them the souls of everyone who moved into your house.

If the spiders are still alive...what have they been eating?

At that moment, you hear a familiar screech. From under the door and through the cracks in the walls, tiny hungry spiders flood into the room!

The End

The gigantic spider wraps Fang up in her web. The sacks that you thought were dust are actually eggs. The mother spider announces *"Dinner!"* to her brood with a shrill screech. The egg sacks screech back. The spider grabs Fang's head in her spindly legs. *Crack!* Fang's head pops off like the cap off of a soda bottle. There is no way you can save her now.

"RUN!" you scream and the three of you tear out of the room. You get out of the room just as the egg sacks are hatching. Tiny hungry spiders cover the walls and floor of the corridor. You try to light as many on fire as you can. You don't even know in what direction you're headed. You just keep running. You look behind you but you don't see Astrid or Alley Cat. You turn into another room and press yourself into the farthest corner.

You feel the serrated edges of insect legs against the back of your head. You spin around and come face to face with another, even bigger spider. You stare into his red eyes for a breathless moment. Then one of his black legs knocks the torch out of your hand and he charges, swallowing you whole.

The End

ABOUT THE ARTIST

Illustrator: Gabhor Utomo was born in Indonesia. He moved to California to pursue his passion in art. He received his degree from the Academy of Art University in San Francisco in Spring 2003. Since graduation, he's worked as a freelance illustrator and has illustrated a number of children's books. Gabhor lives with his wife, Dina, and his twin girls in the San Francisco Bay Area.

ABOUT THE AUTHOR

C. E. Simpson is a native New Yorker living in Brooklyn. She has worked as a playwright for the Flea Theater and WNYC's Greene Space, as a performance artist in an immersive year-round haunted house, and as a set designer. She lived with the Tlingit tribe in Klukwan, Alaska and studied exorcisms and witch craft in Madagascar.

**For games, activities and other fun stuff,
or to write to C. E. Simpson,
visit us online at CYOA.com**

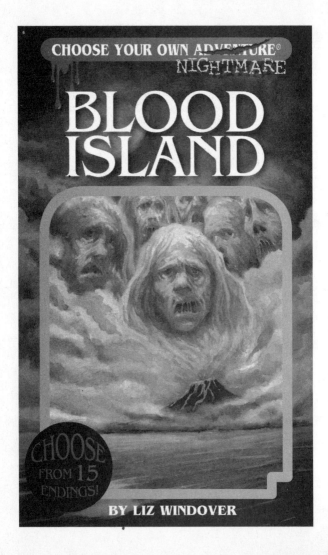